ISBN 978-1-338-68154-3

10 9 8 7 6 5 4 3 2 1   20 21 22 23 24

Made in Jefferson City, USA   40

First printing 2020

Scholastic Inc., 557 Broadway,
New York, NY 10012

Scholastic UK Ltd., Euston House,
24 Eversholt Street, London NW1 1DB

Scholastic LTD, Unit 89E, Lagan Road,
Dublin Industrial Estate, Glasnevin, Dublin 11

THE ULTIMATE PARTY

BY MOLLIE FREILICH

SCHOLASTIC INC.

*B*zzz! *Bzzz! Bzzz!*

"Ahhhhhhh!"

The sound of my alarm clock jolted me out of bed, and I threw my covers across the room in the process. You might be wondering why I set an alarm on a Saturday morning. It wasn't a school day, it wasn't my birthday, and we didn't have a family road trip planned. It was for a way more exciting reason: That morning, at exactly 7:00 a.m. Eastern Standard Time, the Ace Savvy Fan Club was letting a select few fans know the premiere date of the newest movie in the Ace universe, *Ace Savvy and One-Eyed Jack 4: Fur of a Kind*. My best friend, Clyde, and I had been waiting for this day to come for *weeks*. We'd even synchronized our watches yesterday to make sure we logged on to the website at the exact same time.

You may be wondering why it was such a big deal. It's just a movie, right? Wrong! This wasn't just any regular old movie—not only would our all-time favorite villain, The Kitty, return to fight Ace and Jack, but the premiere was going to be right here in Royal Woods!

I turned on my computer and rubbed my eyes.

"C'mon . . . C'mon . . . C'mon! Please load!" I said to my computer as I watched the spinning wheel on-screen turn. I panicked and considered calling Clyde on the walkie-talkie to see if his computer was loading faster, but I remembered his dads started a no-walkie-talkie-before-9-a.m.-unless-it's-an-emergency policy. Just as I was about to declare this to be an emergency worthy of calling, I heard the sweet sound of the Ace and Jack theme song coming out of my computer speakers.

"Yessssss!" I exclaimed as the page finished loading.

I couldn't believe it. Ace and Jack were really coming to Royal Woods. And, most important, the premiere was far enough in the future that I might actually have a chance to go. I immediately opened my door and dashed downstairs as quickly (and as quietly) as I could.

Here's the thing: In a family with eleven kids, we have to keep track of all of our activities on a family calendar. It's the only way our parents can handle all of our busy schedules and find time to plan things like doctor's appointments or family vacations.

So, if you *don't* write down the important stuff you want to do, there's a good chance you won't get to do it. If you forget to write an important event on the calendar, for example, a trip to Aunt Ruth's or an appointment with Dr. Feinstein may be scheduled on the same day Gus's Games & Grubs is having a two-for-one special on pizza and game tokens. Let me tell you: There's nothing worse than getting a teeth cleaning when you know you could be playing the latest *Muscle Fish* game instead.

I grabbed a pen from the junk drawer as I slid across the kitchen floor in my socks. I flipped the calendar ahead a couple of months and sighed with relief when I saw the date of the big premiere was blank. As I wrote the event down, I took my time to make sure each letter was perfectly readable. The second most important rule about the family calendar is making sure you write your thing down clearly. One time, I wrote something down too quickly and neither of my parents could figure out what it said, so they planned a big spring-cleaning day at the house that all of us had to help out with. I was the only kid in my whole class who missed Girl Jordan's bowling and sundae-making party. While my friends were sampling fancy ice-cream flavors, I was polishing the dining table.

Relieved by my scheduling win, I let out a big breath as the calendar fell back to show this month. It was a wild animal–themed calendar—we each get a turn picking out the calendar for the year, and this year had been Lana's choice.

"I wonder what's going on in the Loud house today," I said as I found today's date under the image of puppy-eyed meerkats. I gasped. "Wait, does that say *anniversary*?"

Right between scribbled plans of Leni's shift at Reininger's department store, Luan's stand-up set, and Luna's jam sesh with her band was the word *anniversary*. It's not one of

Lori's anniversaries with Bobby—they had to get a separate calendar for that. (How many pizzaversaries can one couple have, you might ask? Apparently enough to fill up their own calendar.) It wasn't my best-friendiversary with Clyde, either. That was last month.

That could mean only one thing: It must be my parents' anniversary!

I quietly ran back up the stairs and into my bedroom. I paced back and forth, thinking about the calendar. The word *anniversary* was so tiny, and it was hidden by so many other activities. It looked like Lynn had fifty different games scheduled for today alone. (How many sports teams can Lynn be on, anyway?)

I wondered if my parents even remembered it was today and if they had made any plans to celebrate.

The story of my parents' first date is a Loud family legend. Back before any of us were born, my mom was a crossing guard right here in Royal Woods, and every day, my dad crossed that street. He was always singing or speaking in a British accent—some things never change—and my mom totally had a crush on him. My mom was too scared to talk to my dad, so she started slipping secret admirer notes in his pocket when he walked by. In the third note my mom gave my dad, she asked him to meet her at Bangers and Mosh, the local British-themed restaurant and rock venue, for their very first date. They've been together ever since.

My sisters and I have *never* successfully celebrated our parents' anniversary, no matter how hard we've tried. There was the pancake pickle incident, the situation with the potato peeler and the bubble bath, and that one year that led to Dad needing his bottom right molar replaced. No matter what we do or how far in advance we plan, we just can't seem to get the whole celebrating thing right.

After our parents had to replace the shower pipes last year, we vowed that we'd never try to throw them a party again . . . but my scheduling win was giving me a good feeling. I looked at the Ace Savvy poster on my wall. My parents bought that poster for me. They gave me the allowance that paid for my first *Ace Savvy* comic book. They drove me to all the conventions, helped me make my own costume, and once, my mom dressed up as One-Eyed Jack so I could have a sidekick with me while Clyde was home sick. Basically, without my parents, I wouldn't be so ding-dang excited this morning.

And the wild thing was, they didn't just get *me* into *my* stuff, they did that for all eleven of us kids all the time. They were always taking us everywhere and supporting our interests. Our parents did so much for us, and it was time we did something for them in return. We could show them how thankful we were by throwing them an amazing anniversary party! No, it had to be better than amazing—it had to be *epic*. Or even *better* than epic!

I caught my reflection in the window.

"I am Lincoln Loud," I said to my reflection. "I'm the man with the plan! Today is going to be an awesome day. Today is the day I throw the ultimate anniversary party for my parents!" I thought for a minute, then added, "But . . . how do I do that? And in less than one day?"

I looked at my stuffed bunny, Bun-Bun. He slumped over on the bed. Some help he was.

I glanced at the clock. It wasn't even 8 a.m., but I couldn't wait for 9 a.m. to roll around to call Clyde. This definitely qualified as an emergency. Then again, I could wake up my sisters and call them together for a family meeting. I wasn't sure which I should do. Calling Clyde might upset his dads, but Lola once cut a chunk of Lori's hair while she was sleeping because Lori had accidentally woken her up fifteen minutes before she'd finished getting her beauty sleep.

I paced around some more and then pulled

a dry-erase board and marker out from under my bed. The most important part of being the man with the plan is being able to come up with a plan, so I figured I'd brainstorm some ideas before getting anyone else involved.

"**LINCOLN LOUD'S PLAN FOR THE ULTIMATE PARTY**," I wrote at the top of the board.

I thought about what actually makes a party *ultimate*.

It's not really a party at all without people there, I thought as I tapped the marker against the dry-erase board. It would be really great if I could get all of my parents' friends to come, but I'd definitely need help with putting together a list. And you can't just have people standing around doing nothing at a party, so I'd need to find some kind of entertainment.

And there should probably be at least some snacks. I popped the cap off of my marker and jotted down a list on the dry-erase board.

GUEST LIST
ENTERTAINMENT
FOOD
DECORATIONS
VENUE
MUSIC
GIFTS

I looked over my work. With the right combination of all those things, I could totally throw the ultimate party for my parents, but there was no way I could do it all alone. I checked the clock again. Barely any time had passed—it was still way too early to wake up my sisters or call Clyde—but I had to do it. I grabbed the walkie-talkie and pushed the button.

"Cadet Clyde, come in. This is Cadet Lincoln. I have a Code Boysenberry," I said into the microphone. "Repeat: I have a Code Boysenberry. Over."

"This is Cadet Clyde. A Code Boysenberry? You ran out of socks and your washing machine is broken but you have a family photo shoot today? I'm sorry, Lincoln. I just don't think I can break my dads' rule about using the walkie-talkies this early for that," Clyde responded.

"Clyde, that's a Code Raspberry."

"You have to construct a birdhouse from scratch before class tomorrow but the last time you tried working with wood, you glued it to your hand?"

"*No*, Clyde. That's a Code Plum."

"Oh, right. Hmm . . . OK, a Code Boy-senberry . . . Oh no! Today is your parents' anniversary and, despite their warnings against it, you're insisting on throwing them a party because you want a way to express your gratitude?"

"Yes! That's the one!"

"That *is* an emergency!" I could almost hear Clyde starting to hyperventilate.

"Can you help me? You're really good at this kind of stuff."

"I'd love to help you, but first I have to help my dads deliver a coffee table to Nana Gayle. I'll be back in a couple of hours and I'll be ready and willing to help then. What about asking your sisters? Have you tried calling a sibling meeting?"

"I haven't yet. It's so early. You know how Lola gets if I wake her up before her alarm clock goes off."

"That's true. That scar I have from when she bit my hand never did properly heal."

"And Lynn could totally pound me if I woke her up at the wrong time," I said, rubbing my shoulder.

"Isn't the pounding worth the risk?"

"Maybe I should just try to do this by myself."

"Lincoln, there's no way you're throwing a party for your parents without your sisters! Most of your family is your sisters, and you can't celebrate your parents without having most of your family involved. I'm an only child and even I know that!"

I sighed. "You're right, Clyde. But what if they all get mad at me?"

"Then you'll deal with that later. You've got this! You're Lincoln Loud! You can wake up your sisters without them being angrier than you've ever seen them in your life!"

"I sure hope you're right, Clyde."

"I know I'm right. Listen, I gotta go. I'll call you when I'm back!"

"Thanks, Clyde. Over and out," I said as I tossed the walkie-talkie onto my bed.

Clyde was right. I needed my sisters' help, otherwise the party would be a total disaster. Even if I knew exactly what needed to be done, I'd still need people to actually *do* the things that needed to be done.

I opened my door and entered the hallway. It was time to call a very early sibling meeting.

I took a deep breath. *There's no time to lose*, I thought as I braced myself for my sisters' reactions. My hand shook as I raised it up to make a door-knocking fist. I'd never been so afraid to hit a piece of wood in my whole life.

"Sibling meeting! Sibling meeting!" I whisper-shouted as I knocked on each door.

I needed to wake my sisters up, but I definitely did not want to wake up my parents downstairs in the process. One by one, each of my sisters popped into their doorways.

"What is the meaning of this abrupt suspension of my sweet REM cycle?" my sister Lisa asked.

"Baa! Poo-poo!" her roommate Lily agreed as she waved her tiny hands.

"YOU ARE RUINING MY BEAUTY SLEEP!" Lola screamed. Her face was covered in a green mask, so she looked like an angry monster. I flinched and raised my finger to my mouth to shush her, but she was not having it. "DON'T YOU *SHH* ME! YOU KNOW I NEED EIGHT FULL HOURS!"

"What's the deal, Stinkin'? It's Saturday," Lynn said gruffly.

"Yeah, brah," Luna chimed in from her doorway. "I'm trying to have some dreams over here."

"Lincoln, you are literally interrupting my hourly video chat with Bobby," Lori said, her cell phone clutched tightly. "Why are you running around to call a sibling meeting this early on a Saturday morning?"

I gulped. Had I made a mistake?

"Spit it out, Lincoln!" my sisters shouted at the same time.

"You guys, it's Mom and Dad's anniversary today. I want us to get together and plan the ultimate anniversary party for them."

My sisters all groaned.

"No way," Luna said.

"Not a chance," Lola said.

"Uh-uh, absolutely not," Luan said.

"I know it's super last minute, but we owe it to them. They do so much for us. Come on. Lola, who always gets the special sparkly stick-on earrings you like?"

"Mom and Dad," Lola replied, checking her manicure.

"And Luna, who drove you to every guitar lesson and still goes to all of your gigs, even if they're way out in Hazeltucky?"

"Mom and Pop-star, of course," Luna replied.

"And Luan," I started.

"We get it, Lincoln. We think Mom and Dad are great, too, but we all know we're not supposed to do *anything* for their anniversary anymore," Luan said. "Well, not after that whole mix-up with the herring and the blow-torch. Talk about a *red herring*! Ha-ha-ha, get

it? But seriously, we shouldn't throw a party."

"I know, but we've never really worked *together* on figuring out a plan before," I pleaded. I couldn't give up before even trying! "I've been thinking about it all morning. If everyone takes on one small task each, we'll be able to bring those things together and pull off a party unlike anything Mom and Dad have ever seen. But we can only do it if we all work together. Right now, I'm just asking for a second of your time to listen to my plan. If you like the plan, awesome! We throw the ultimate party. If not, well . . ." I looked down at my feet. "At least I tried."

"Why didn't you say so?" Lori asked with a smile. "You really are the Master of Convincing, Lincoln. C'mon—everyone, inside."

She opened the door to the room she shares

with our sister Leni, and my sisters shuffled in, grumbling. I dashed quickly to my room at the other end of the hall to retrieve my dry-erase board. Inside Lori and Leni's bedroom, I felt twenty eyes on me all at once, and most of them did not look happy.

I can do this. I'm the man with the plan. I can do this! I thought.

Hey, sometimes even the Master of Convincing needs to be convinced.

"As you know, we have made several attempts to celebrate our parents in the past, and we've yet to succeed," I began. "Earlier this morning, as I was adding a very important future plan to the family calendar, I discovered that today is their anniversary—"

"We get it, Stinkin'! Out with the plan already!" Lynn interrupted.

Sometimes, it doesn't matter how good your plan might be, because you might find yourself surrounded by ten sisters who would rather be doing anything else on a Saturday morning other than listening to you. Then you totally panic, and your perfect plan goes totally off the rails.

I looked at my dry-erase board, and it seemed like it was written in a different language. When I was making my list earlier, I'd thought about which of us would be the best at each task. But in that moment, my legs turned to jelly and my mind went completely blank. So, I improvised—badly.

"You want a plan? I have a plan! I have t-t-tons of plans," I stuttered, trying to buy myself time to remember who was supposed to do what.

"Lincoln!" my sisters yelled simultaneously.

"OK, Lynn, you're in charge of entertainment."

"All right!" Lynn replied. She quickly pulled on her lucha libre mask and pumped her fist.

"Lisa, you're . . . ummm . . . you're handling the guest list."

"Preposterous!" Lisa cried, crossing her arms.

"Leni, you're on food."

"Ugh! Where?!" Leni squealed, checking under her feet. The rest of us sighed and shook our heads.

I continued my assignments. "Um, Lori, you and Lana are in charge of food."

"You literally just said Leni was on food," Lori replied.

"We'll be fine, Lori!" Lana said, pulling some dirt out of the pocket of her pajamas. "I just got a fresh batch of mud pies in from Tall Timbers Pond!"

Uh-oh. This was not going well. "Dang it!" I cried. "I mean, Lori and Lana are on entertainment!"

"What gives?" Lynn asked, tugging her lucha libre mask back up.

"I, uhhhh . . ." The room spun around me. I felt a hand tap my shoulder.

"Don't worry, I've got this," Lori said to me. "OK, you guys, if we're going to throw a party, there's only one way to do it: According to *Seventeen and a Half* magazine, the best parties always have the most sophisticated snacks. So we should totally make them rose-shaped kale chips!"

"Mom doesn't even like kale," Lola said. "Also, I'm pretty sure the last time you tried to take that magazine's tips to throw a party, it was a total snooze-factory."

"Like you have any better ideas?"

"Of course I do. I wasn't named Little Miss Party Planner of Lower Michigan for nothing!"

"Didn't you lose that pageant to Lindsay Sweetwater?" Lucy asked.

"TAKE IT BACK!" Lola screamed.

"You wouldn't know how to plan a party if it popped out of a coffin in the middle of a cemetery, Lucy!" Luan chimed in.

"At least at the cemetery, the comedians have better jokes," Lucy retorted.

"You guys, we just have to design a bunch

of fun outfits for Mom and Dad. If they're looking good and feeling good, that will be more than enough celebration!" Leni said.

"Can it, fashionista! What Mom and Dad really need is some high-intensity training!" Lynn said.

"You wouldn't know what Mom and Dad really need if it bit you on the butt!" Lana yelled.

Before I knew it, all of my sisters were arguing with one another. I'm pretty sure I heard one of them blame me for something that happened before I was even born. It got pretty wild—even though we were all in pajamas, I had to duck to avoid at least three shoes chucked through the air. Luckily, we hadn't yet woken our parents up, but I knew my plan to throw the ultimate party was totally ruined.

"Come on, you guys! We have to work together! Don't fight!" I shouted over the noise, dodging an incoming tiara.

My sisters stopped quickly. I suddenly had twenty eyes on me again—this time, looking even unhappier than before.

"Lincoln's right," Lori said. "We should

stop fighting. We shouldn't be mad at each other—we should be mad at him!"

"Yeah!" the rest of my sisters agreed. "This is Lincoln's fault!"

Gulp. "You've got it all wrong!" I said. "We're just having some trouble working together. Listen, I'll go back and figure out exactly who can do what, and when *that* plan is ready, I'll—"

"I'm going back to bed," Luna interrupted, then opened the door to leave Lori and Leni's room. "Sorry, brah. I'd rather do nothing than risk totally ruining another anniversary for Mom and Dad."

"Wait for me, toots! I could use more shut-eye, too!" Luan called out from behind Luna, talking as her dummy, Mr. Coconuts.

The rest of my sisters filed out of Lori

and Leni's room, grumbling on the way.

"I cannot believe you woke me up for this," Lola said. "Do you know what yelling this early in the morning is going to do for my hair? I can feel the oils building up already." She flipped her hair and huffed out the door.

"If this disturbance in my sleep causes bruxism, you'll be hearing from my dentist," Lisa said, carrying Lily with her. Lily blew a raspberry at me. I was lucky she didn't throw her diaper.

"Sorry, Lincoln," Leni said. "Maybe we can do something for Mom and Dad next year?"

I hung my head. So much for my big plan. I should've known that it would be impossible for all of us to do something so big at the last minute. I thought about all the things I should've done differently. As I walked down the hall to my room, my mind wandered. I wasn't really paying attention to where I was going, and nearly tripped over my sister Lynn's foot.

"Watch it, Stinkin'!"

"Sorry, Lynn," I said, looking up. Standing in front of me were Lynn, Lucy, and Lana. "Wait, what are you all doing out in the hall still? I thought you were all going back to sleep."

"We were thinking," Lana said. "It *would* be really cool to do something nice for Mom and Dad. They haven't seen my bug circus in months, and we've finally perfected Charlie and Karina's trapeze act! Besides, we're already awake."

Lucy added solemnly, "When I last spoke

to the spirit of Great-Grandma Harriet, she advised I pitch in the next time the moon and the stars cross Mercury. This is that time."

"Yeah, and my field hockey practice I was supposed to go to today got canceled, so I need to crank out all this extra energy somehow!" Lynn said, lifting the hall table—vase and all—up over her head. "Plus, it's probably time I do something for Mom and Dad, especially after the whole spicy mustard episode."

This was a surprise! But I was happy to go with it.

"Uh, OK! Let's do this!" I said. Hey, maybe we wouldn't be able to pull off the *ultimate* party for our parents, but we could at least try to do something for them. And having three sisters to help was definitely better than having none. At least, I *hoped* it would be.

"OK, Stinkin'," Lynn grunted, cracking her knuckles. "What's the game plan?"

I looked at my list on the dry-erase board and thought about my ultimate party plan. We definitely couldn't do everything I'd listed, but we could probably handle the most important things. Maybe?

"Well, when I was thinking about it before, all eleven of us were involved," I said.

"I didn't think there'd only be four of us. I have an idea of how we can make this party happen, but it feels pretty impossible right now."

"You sound a little sad, bro. Are you sure you want to plan a whole party?" Lana asked. "I could just have my crickets perform for you as a cheer-up thing. You'll love it. When they start juggling frozen peas, the fun really gets going."

"Or we could only invite guests from beyond," Lucy suggested. "I'm sure Great-Grandma Harriet has some people in mind."

"I don't know, you guys. Maybe this isn't such a good idea," I said. Maybe Lana was right, and a whole party was too much.

"Lincoln, if you really want to win, you need to have the winning spirit," Lynn said. "If you

keep thinking and acting like a loser, we're going to lose. This is your winning team." She gestured to Lana and Lucy. "We're basically the first-round draft picks of the family. We're your point guards! We're your closing pitchers!"

Lynn chest-bumped me hard, and I flew backward. It must've knocked me out of my negative thinking, because as I got up, I had an idea. Sure, this group of my sisters wasn't the most ideal group for party planning—unless the party's theme was mud, sports, or Goth—but they're all really good at getting stuff done.

"What's the plan, Lincoln?" Lucy asked.

"Originally, I was thinking about re-creating Mom and Dad's first date at Bangers and Mosh downstairs," I started.

"Oooh! Good idea!" my sisters said.

"Buuuut . . . there is no way the three of us can do that by ourselves. So, we'll have to stick to what we all do best."

"That sounds like a great idea, Linc, but the number of mud pies I can make in such a short time really depends on the number of guests and—"

"No, Lana, that's not really what I had in mind."

"So what *were* you thinkin', Stinkin'?"

"I've got it," I said. "Lynn, you're responsible for getting party food. Remember: Anything you like that's even a little spicy, make it like eight thousand times less spicy than you would normally."

"Got it," Lynn said. She pulled a marker out of her pocket and wrote on her arm. "Chumps.

Can't. Handle. Heat. BOOYAH! Done!" She put the cap back on the marker and spiked it like a football.

I turned to my next sister. "We might not be able to re-create a two-story British dining establishment and concert venue, but we can make the house look nice, and that's the next best thing. Lucy, you've got a bunch of flower shop connections from the funeral services the Morticians Club provides, right? Can you maybe get some last-minute flower arrangements so we can have some decorations?"

"I wrote the obituary for Sachi the florist's cat last week. I'll ask her."

"Great. Lana, that leaves you."

"Say no more, Lincoln," Lana said. "You need some top-quality entertainment."

"Um, I don't know, Lans," I said. "Maybe there's something else you can do?"

"Trust me. I get that you're not a bug guy, but I've gotta say, this new batch of crickets Hops and I have been working is really talented, and I *know* they will impress you. We even built a tiny unicycle for the finale."

"This isn't like the termite disco, is it?"

"No, totally different. Chester can't dance."

It wasn't the perfect plan, but it was *a* plan. And what other option did we have?

"OK, Lana. Go for it. Get your crickets in order."

"Let's do this, guys! Hands in!" Lynn shouted. The four of us stood in a circle and stacked our hands in the center. "*Loud and proud* on three. Ready? One, two, three!"

"LOUD AND PROUD!" we all shouted. (Well, except for Lucy. Lucy said it in her usual Lucy way with her usual Lucy level of energy.) It was time to get started!

We all changed out of our pajamas and met downstairs in the dining room to figure out what we needed. I was in charge of the guest list and running party-planning-related errands.

While we had been planning upstairs, our parents had gotten up and left the house with our youngest sister, Lily. I checked the family calendar. Lily had her Diaper Dancers class in the morning, and then my parents had a list of errands to handle, scrawled in tiny letters under everyone else's activities. The list was long and included things like washing the car and dropping off Mom's latest article for the newspaper, so they'd be out for at least a few hours. We had *just* enough time to pull off planning a party. Everything was coming together.

Lynn decided she was going to make meatball subs. She even promised to lay off on the hot sauce this time. Lucy was going to pick up flowers from Sachi the florist. Sure, they were used at a funeral yesterday, but it wasn't a time for us to be picky. And Lana was drawing a blueprint for her cricket circus—complete with flying trapeze.

"I'm going to go to Flip's to pick up some ice cream for dessert and a card for Mom and Dad that we can get everyone to sign," I said. "I should be back home in about an hour. When I come home, I'll help you guys finish and try to get the rest of our sisters to come celebrate with us. Maybe I can even call Pop-Pop and Myrtle. I bet they'd come over, too!"

"Sounds good, Lincoln. We've got everything under control here!" Lana said. She high-fived her frog Hops's tongue.

I left my sisters and rode my bike down to Flip's Food and Fuel. As I pedaled, I made a mental list of people I could invite to our smaller, but still pretty great, party. My grandpa Pop-Pop and his girlfriend, Myrtle (also known as Gran-Gran), would definitely come over. I could probably trade one of my dad's famous

Lynn-sagnas to my neighbor Mr. Grouse in exchange for him making an appearance, Clyde and his dads would definitely come if they were available, and, of course, our sisters would show up once we'd proven that the party was problem-free.

I imagined how surprised my parents would be when they came home to our celebration. My dad would take a bite out of a meatball sub and tears of happiness would drip down his face. My mom would sniff the flowers and smile, and she'd compliment Lana on her cricket's triple flip. My Pop-Pop would make a joke and the whole room would burst into a fit of laughter. Our whole family would share a big hug and my parents would say, "Thanks, kids, this was the best anniversary ever." One of my sisters, maybe Lori, would tell them it was my idea to throw the party. I'd say we all did it together, and the sisters who didn't help set up would do my chores over the next couple of weeks to make up for doubting that we could pull off throwing a party. It wouldn't be the biggest or the best party, but it would be pretty dang close to perfect.

Oops! I was so lost in thought that I nearly rode past Flip's! I hopped off my bike and walked into the store with new confidence. I found the greeting card section of the store and thumbed through the tiny selection.

"'Ey, Chief!" Flip yelled at me from behind the counter. "This ain't a library! You read it, you buy it."

"Just looking for the right card for my parents!"

"They're all the right card!"

"That doesn't even make any sense," I said aloud to myself.

The only greeting cards he had were for: an uncle-specific birthday, St. Patrick's Day, grandparent-specific Arbor Day, celebrating a cat adoption, and something called Cheese Appreciation Day. I figured the cat adoption card was the best option. On the front, it had a cat with big eyes and the word "Congratulations!" Inside the card, it said, "Your new friend is a 'purr-fect' match for you!" My sister Luan would love the pun inside. At least it was cute.

Next, I checked out the ice-cream options. I quickly wished I'd ridden my bike a little longer and gone to the supermarket instead, but I knew I didn't have time for that trip, and had to move fast. There was still so much to do! Inside the ice-cream case, there were a few scattered Popsicles that looked like they'd melted at some point and been thrown back in the case. There were only two cartons of ice cream that were family-sized (or even a little shareable, for that matter). One of the cartons clearly looked like it had been opened—Flip is known for snacking on his own supply—so I took the other one. I guess a sealed carton of vanilla with chocolate-covered pickles and rainbow sprinkles ice cream was better than no dessert.

I paid Flip and hopped back on my bike. I raced back to my house so I could help Lana, Lucy, and Lynn set up for the party. Even though my contribution wasn't exactly perfect, my sisters' stuff seemed like it would be on track for success.

I parked my bike and opened the front door—and my jaw dropped.

"YOU GUYS!" I yelled. "WHAT HAPPENED?!"

It was chaos—way more than the usual level of Loud family chaos. In the corner of the living room, there were black curtains hung on the walls behind a giant, creaky pipe organ. On top of the organ was Lucy's bat, Fangs, and a bunch of his bat friends. The bats were shrieking along to the tune on the pipe organ, which rattled my eardrums.

Instead of flowers, Lana was attaching balloons made of ABC (as in, Already Been Chewed) gum and doggie poop bags (thankfully unused) to the walls. It was worse than the time she and Lucy were in charge of decorating for our mom's birthday, when the living room had been covered in toilet paper and whatever Lana could find in her pockets and under her bed, and Lana had crafted belly-button lint and booger table settings that were about as gross as you could imagine. (We ended up scrapping that idea before Mom got home.)

Now the living room floor was lined with old car tires leading all the way into the dining room, because Lynn was in the middle of setting up an obstacle course.

"We were out of ingredients for the subs," Lynn said with a shrug. "So, I built this sick obstacle course. Mom and Dad can compete to see who gets through it the fastest. That's how I'd want to celebrate. Plus, you asked me to avoid making anything spicy."

Lana came over. "The crickets didn't feel they were 'performance-ready,' and I've found it's better to let them make those kinds of choices for themselves," she said. "Plus, the flower shop is on the other side of town, so we realized Lucy wouldn't be able to get there and back in time to set everything up. I had these poop bags for Charles just sitting around, so we thought we'd put them to good use!"

One of Fangs's bat friends screeched and

dive-bombed my hair, nearly knocking my turkey tail off. This wasn't a party—this was a disaster! I knew my sisters were trying their best, but at the same time, it felt like they weren't taking this party seriously.

"This is a mess," I said. "You guys need to clean this all up."

"What?! We worked really hard on this!" Lana said. A gum-balloon popped on the wall.

Lucy sighed. "I had to call in a favor with Bertrand to get this organ all the way here," she protested.

"We can't possibly throw a party for Mom and Dad that looks like this," I replied, pointing to all the gross and weird stuff around the room.

"What do you mean? Everyone enjoys pipe organ music," Lucy said.

"Yeah! And everyone enjoys gum and poop bags!" Lana added.

"You know what? We need to start over. Let's get rid of all this junk and start from scratch," I said.

My sisters looked at me like I had destroyed all of their most-prized possessions at the same time. I knew it must've been hurtful for them to hear that we had to get rid of everything they had already done, but Mom and Dad's party had to be the priority.

"Wow. Nice one, Lincoln," Lana said sarcastically.

"Thanks a lot, Stinkin'." Lynn lifted a tire over her head. "I've had enough. If anyone's looking for me, I'll be doing push-ups in the backyard until I chill out."

"I can't believe we wasted our Saturday

morning *and* my pre-chewed gum collection for this," Lana said. She peeled a wad of gum off the wall and popped it into her mouth. "Come on, Luce. Let's go help Lynn count off her push-ups and dig some holes in the backyard."

"Wait! You guys! We can fix this!" I called after them.

"Good luck with *your* party, Lincoln."

"Bye, Lincoln."

My sisters left through the kitchen door. Fangs and his friends followed them in a swarm, nearly knocking me over. Everything was a mess. I felt guilty for making my sisters feel bad, and I was totally freaking out. I was right back to where I started this morning, but the clock was ticking, time was almost up, and I had no help.

I surveyed the room and tried to salvage whatever I could from my sisters' decorations. I pulled down one of the poop-bag balloons, then twisted it in my hands to try to make it look like a flower or something. *Maybe I could tie them together and make streamers*, I thought. But everything I tried to do with them just looked more and more like trash. I knew one of my sisters would've been able to make these look nice, but I couldn't make it happen alone.

I gave up on trying to make the poop bags look like anything other than what they actually were and walked over to the pipe organ. *Maybe I have time to write a song for our parents*, I thought. *How hard can it be to write a song?* I touched one of the keys on the organ. It produced a sound so loud, I tripped backward over the couch and fell into one of the tires Lynn had set up for her obstacle course.

"WELL, THAT IDEA IS OUT," I shouted to myself over my ringing ears.

It was clear I wouldn't be able to turn the current situation into the ultimate anniversary party without making some drastic changes. So I rushed through the living room and dining room and cleaned up as much as I could. The only things I left were a stack of tires (I had no idea where Lynn got them, anyway) and the giant pipe organ.

I rummaged through the fridge and the cupboards to look for food that could be used for party snacks. No wonder Lynn gave up on the subs—there was barely enough food to make two deviled eggs and half a sandwich. I took a glance at the family calendar, and sure enough, it was grocery day. Mom and Dad would be going to the market on their way home today. That also explained why Dad's "Famous Leftover Casserole" was particularly strange last night—it doesn't usually include a can of Aunt Ruth's expired wartime pudding.

I couldn't go to the market myself, though. For one thing, if I ran into my parents, they would figure out what I was up to and would probably try to stop me. (One of the times we tried to throw a party for them, Leni accidentally used salt instead of sugar in the cake and Dad's taste buds didn't work right for a week afterward, so our parents prefer that we don't try to cook for them ever again.) The other thing was, I didn't really have any money—or a whole lot of time. I think Flip could smell how desperate I was when I'd bought the ice cream and the card earlier, because he added some kind of "stressed kid" tax. I didn't have the energy to fight him, but I really could've used that extra three dollars.

So, going to the grocery store was out. How was I going to get snacks for the party?

Just then, I heard a noise that sounded like metal scraping concrete, and I ran outside.

"Hey, Loud!"

It was our grumpy next-door neighbor, Mr. Grouse. The sound I'd heard was a three-wheeled skateboard skidding across the driveway after Mr. Grouse had chucked it over his wall. He was in his gardening gear and looked pretty upset.

"Hi, Mr. Grouse," I said, picking up the skateboard.

"Loud! Your rolling board doodad was in my ding-dang begonias!"

"I'm sorry, Mr. Grouse."

"You kids need to be more careful. Maybe you should try respecting your elders," he said with a huff.

That gave me an idea. Sure, Mr. Grouse was constantly annoyed by us (well, all of us except Lynn, his sports-watching buddy), but he had to respect that wanting to throw a party for our parents was a way of respecting our elders, right?

"Say, Mr. Grouse, your trillium flowers are looking particularly nice," I said with a huge smile.

"Whaddya want, Loud?" Mr. Grouse asked suspiciously.

"Well, today is my parents' anniversary and—"

"I'm going to stop you right there," he

interrupted. "I heard some of the caterwauling coming from some of you kids in the yard and I am *not* allowing a buncha cricket clowns on my property."

"Actually, the crickets weren't feeling performance-ready," I said. Mr. Grouse got up from the flower bed and walked to his door. "Wait! I'm just trying to gather some snacks so I can throw a party for my parents!"

"You're on your own for that one. Besides, your dad owes me two of his Lynn-sagnas after that dog of yours took a number two in my rosebush."

"Please, Mr. Grouse. It's an emergency!"

"Look, Loud," Mr. Grouse said, his voice softened. "Why don't you just get them a gift card to that restaurant they like so much. What's that one? The one where they had their first date? Boomers and Slosh?"

"Bangers and Mosh."

"Same thing," he said.

"What if I could get you three of his Lynn-sagnas?"

"Your dad's already late on getting the first two to me. Adding another invisible lasagna isn't going to help your case. Like I said, kid: You're on your own. Just get 'em the gift card and call it a day."

Mr. Grouse went inside his house and closed the door. Dang it.

I had to admit he'd had a good idea: Getting a gift card to Bangers and Mosh would be the next best thing to throwing a really good party. But I was out of money and I couldn't bear to ask my sisters to chip in. Three of them were definitely mad at me, six of them were probably mad at me, and one of them didn't even know how to count to ten yet. I had to think of another plan.

I considered going back to Flip's so I could trade the ice cream for some nachos, but then I realized I wouldn't have any dessert, and it's a proven fact that all good parties have dessert.

I went back inside the house and started pac-
ing. *Think, Lincoln, think!* I considered the
limited options I had. Without any money,
going to the mall to get my parents a really cool
gift was out of the question. Plus, the last time
my sisters and I tried to get my dad a gift at the
mall, we realized our parents don't really love

store-bought stuff anyway. We'd made him a scrapbook, but then Lori told us about the super-cool gift her friend Carol Pingrey got for *her* dad and we totally freaked out. We'd almost found him a good gift, but nothing worked out: A glass dolphin turned out to be a porpoise (and my dad has a bad history with porpoises); a Beefeater nutcracker would've been great, but Dad's best friend, Kotaro, got a *real* Beefeater to come over for the day; and a personalized spatula would've taken weeks to special order. Finally, we came home empty-handed—but while we were out, our cat, Cliff, accidentally removed our scrapbook from the trash, and we found Dad sobbing tears of joy over how great he thought it was.

My next idea was to go to Pop-Pop's retirement home: Sunset Canyon. I knew they had event space because we celebrated Myrtle's birthday there once, but my parents weren't really into only having food you can eat with a straw. Besides, Sunset Canyon always kind of smelled like cleaning products, and we wouldn't be able to invite anyone over to come celebrate.

We could always have a picnic in the park! I'd still have to find food for us to eat, but at least the space was nice and we could invite people. Then I remembered that Tall Timbers Park had multiple swamp monster sightings. It was worth the risk for my family—it was probably one of my sisters behind the whole swamp monster thing—but I was nervous that other people wouldn't come.

Hmm. The bowling alley? Closed for renovations.

Dairyland? Not really an "anniversary" kind of place.

Jean Juan's French-Mex Buffet? We'd never be able to get a reservation for our big family on a Saturday!

Maybe I couldn't find the right place today . . . but what if everyone thought it was actually still *yesterday*? What if everyone in Royal Woods thought it was Friday instead of Saturday? Sure, I'd have to go to school for another day, but I'd also have another day to plan my parents' anniversary party! I'd just have to somehow turn back everyone's calendar, and . . .

Who was I kidding? Even Leni wouldn't believe it was Friday. Fridays are too exciting. They're the end of the week—the day we all look forward to! Plus, we have so many family activities that end up on Fridays that there's no way our parents would ever buy it.

I looked through my drawers. Maybe I had something I could sell to Flip in exchange for a better party gift. I tossed a pair of old jeans and a broken Starship Groupers toy to the floor. I didn't have a single thing I could trade for the ultimate party experience I was trying to create for my parents. Even my nicest orange polo shirt had a small stain by the collar. I was totally hopeless.

In desperation, I grabbed Bun-Bun. I held him up and considered what I might be able to get for selling him. Then one of his ears flopped and I realized that no party would be worth this kind of sacrifice. I might have to face it. I might be totally incapable of throwing the ultimate anniversary party for my parents.

But maybe going to Flip's could still help, even though I had nothing I could sell him. When we had been looking for the perfect birthday present for my dad, Flip had plenty of things for us to choose from, though they were all expensive and definitely out of my price range. But maybe I could figure something out.

I rode my bike like it was on fire, as fast as I possibly could. I was totally out of breath when I got to Flip's. I took a few deep breaths and rushed inside. Flip was sitting at the counter, reading a newspaper, with his feet in the nacho cheese.

"Ahhh!" he cried, startled. He pulled his feet out of the cheese as soon as he saw me, then composed himself and stared me down. "You didn't see nothin', kid."

"Flip, you know I saw your feet in the nacho

cheese," I said. I'd never tried challenging Flip before. I knew I was risking future Flippees—the greatest slushies on the planet—but it was for a good cause. (I hoped.)

"Like I said, Chief. You. Didn't. See. Nothin'." He stood up. He isn't that much taller than I am, but he reminds me of a villain from an *Ace Savvy* comic.

"I saw your feet in the cheese! Can you give me something for free?" The words flew out of my mouth faster than my brain could work. *What had I done?*

Flip came out from behind the counter.

"You come into Flip's place and you think you can ask Flip for free stuff?"

I nodded quietly.

"You think you can threaten Flip with something like cheese feet?"

"Um, no, sir?" Now I was just confused.

"HA! Get out of my store, kid. In fact, you can't come back here until I tell you. Or, you know, until a grandparent sends you a bunch of money and you feel like buying snacks. Whatever comes first."

Using a Flippee straw, Flip poked me on the back, and I ran out of the store. I didn't know it was possible to get kicked out of Flip's. I've seen Scoots eat a frozen burrito straight out of the package without microwaving it before, and she's never even been kicked out of Flip's.

If anyone should be kicked out of Flip's, it should be Flip! The man had his feet in the cheese, for crying out loud! I was just hoping I'd be able to get my parents *something*—even if it was something stupid, like a car air freshener—and now I was once again empty-handed.

I scrambled back home, and thought about all the future Flippees I'd have to miss. *Would Flip even remember me tomorrow?* I shook my head.

I didn't have time to think about lost Flippees. I was still on a mission.

Exhausted and out of ideas, I fell on my bed. I was ready to give up. My eyes wandered to the latest issue of *Ace Savvy* on my dresser.

"You can do this, Lincoln!"

I rubbed my eyes. It was *Ace* talking to me! He'd popped out of my comic and was standing on my dresser talking to me. I didn't know

I was *that* tired . . . but real or imaginary, I needed someone to talk to, and Ace was there.

"I've tried everything! I can't do it!" I said.

"Did I give up when the Old Maid was holding the whole city hostage?"

"No, but—"

"Did I give up when The Kitty continued to spit hair balls at me when we were in the middle of the greatest car chase in history?"

"No, but—"

"Then why would you give up now, Lincoln? Without your parents, you wouldn't be talking to me right now. Don't they deserve to be showered with gratitude in the form of a totally impossible party?"

"You're right. My parents have given me and my sisters so much. They deserve the *best* party. But I just don't know if I can do it."

"Are you the man with the plan or are you just another kid who can't pull off a super-awesome last-minute party for his parents?"

"I guess."

"Not good enough. Are you the man with the plan or not?!"

"You're right! I'm the man with the plan! I've got this! I can do this!"

I looked back at my dresser, and Ace was gone, but I was full of new energy. There was still time left to make something happen, but like Ace Savvy needing One-Eyed Jack, I knew I couldn't do it alone.

It wasn't time to reach out to my sisters again. I should've been nicer to Lana, Lucy, and Lynn earlier, and I should've had my plan together before calling the sibling meeting this morning. It was just like the time I tried to get my sisters together to take a photo for our parents' anniversary. I'd tried to make them act different and look different, and it totally blew up in my face. I needed a new idea. I needed to get ahold of my One-Eyed Jack.

Then, like magic, I heard the crackle of my walkie-talkie from my dresser.

"Cadet Lincoln, come in. This is Cadet Clyde. We're back from delivering Nana Gayle's table. Do you copy?"

My BFF, Clyde! The One-Eyed Jack to my Ace Savvy! He was back! I grabbed my walkie-talkie and clicked it on to respond.

"Clyde! I'm so happy to hear your voice!"

"How's the party planning going?"

"It's a total disaster. All of my sisters are mad at me, I'm pretty sure I'm banned for life from Flip's, I just talked to an imaginary Ace Savvy, and I'm completely plan-less!"

"The Man with the Plan is plan-less?! What hope do the rest of us have?" I heard Clyde hyperventilate into a paper bag over the walkie. "Wait, did you say you talked to Ace Savvy?"

"Clyde, calm down!"

"OK, OK," Clyde said. "I can be totally calm. I'm the calmest."

"You don't sound very calm."

I heard him take one long, deep breath.

"OK, I'm good. I promise."

"You sure?"

"I'm sure."

"OK, good. Now, do you think you can help me? I know you were busy with your dads earlier, but I could really, really use the help."

"What happened with your sisters?"

"It's a long story. They're all mad at me now. I'm basically an only child."

"Oh no!"

"Yeah, I'm sure I'll be making some big apologies later. But there's no time for that, now! Can you help me?"

"Of course, buddy! What are best friends for? Besides, I've been working on perfecting my recipes for orange-chocolate mousse and pineapple gâteau, and this feels like the perfect occasion to debut their deliciousness."

"Right, totally," I said. I had no idea what pineapple gâteau was, but Clyde is a master chef, so I trusted him. He once made a triple-layer cake that made my dad cry because it was so good. Clyde just has a tendency to talk about stuff, especially food and furniture, in a way that makes it sound like he's from another time. It's probably because he and his dads spend so much time antiquing. Then it hit me. His dads!

Why didn't I think of this before?! I thought, tapping my forehead. "Clyde!"

"Yeah, Lincoln?"

"Do you think your dads would be able to help us? If anyone could help pull together the ultimate anniversary party for my parents, it's them!"

"I don't know, Lincoln. They have a ton of stuff to do today. They have to take the cats for a walk, pick up a baroque credenza from an obscure antique seller in the countryside, *and* they have late-afternoon goat yoga. Dr. Lopez thinks it will get them to connect more with animals and nature."

I sank on my bed.

"Clyde, I'm really in a jam. I've been trying to pull this off all day, and even though together we're Clincoln McCloud, I know the two of us just aren't going to be able to handle this by ourselves."

"OK, I'll ask them," said Clyde. "They *do* love throwing parties and pulling off impossible feats in short amounts of time."

I jumped off my bed and pumped my fist in the air. This party might just happen after all!

"Remember that amazing party they threw together last minute for Mrs. Johnson?" I asked.

"Oh yeah! Teacher Appreciation Week has never felt so festive."

"The apple-shaped confetti was a really nice touch."

"Everyone seemed to love the personalized chalkboard sugar cookies, too," Clyde added.

"You're a real lifesaver, Clyde," I said. "I'll be over there in fifteen minutes."

"Sounds good, Lincoln! See you soon."

I clicked off the walkie-talkie and put it in my backpack along with some supplies and the dry-erase board with my ultimate plan on it. Then I grabbed my bike helmet and ran back downstairs.

I pedaled so fast, I practically flew all the way to Clyde's house. I was full of energy again. I couldn't wait to find out if Clyde's dads said yes to helping us with the party. At least with Clyde's help, the worst-case scenario for celebrating my parents' anniversary would be giving them a fancy dessert as a gift. But if Clyde's dads helped, it would almost be like the last few hours of failure never happened. The slate would be wiped clean! We'd be back on track.

I nearly knocked over the gnome on Clyde's lawn as I jumped off my bike and rang the doorbell. Clyde's dads, Harold and Howard, answered the door together.

"Hi, Lincoln! Come in, come in! Clyde told us all about your soiree predicament," Harold said as I walked through the door.

"I'm not so sure how much we'll be able to help, to be honest. It's such short notice!" Howard, Clyde's slightly more nervous parent, exclaimed.

"Nonsense, Howie. Remember that huge surprise party we planned in three hours back in college? This will be a piece of cake compared to that."

"But that was for a birthday, not an anniversary! We don't even know what anniversary it is! What if it's their sapphire anniversary and we give them silver?!"

"Howie, you're spiraling. Besides, I don't even think Rita is 'sapphire anniversary' years old," Harold said, patting Howard on the shoulder. "Now, Lincoln, what can we do to help you?"

"Thanks, Mr. and Mr. McBride. You see, as I'm sure Clyde told you, my sisters and I stopped trying to celebrate my parents' anniversary because every time we try, it goes totally wrong. But this year, I'd really like to throw the ultimate anniversary party for them."

Howard fainted. Harold put a pillow under his head and guided me to the kitchen.

"Don't worry," Harold said. "He gets like

this about last-minute planning. He'll be fine."

Harold ushered me over to the kitchen table. Clyde was already sitting down with a notepad and pen. Even after all these years of being best friends with him, it's still surprising to see such an organized family. Sometimes in our house, I don't even know where to find a pen.

"Hey, Clyde."

"Hi, Lincoln. Did you come up with any ideas for your parents' party while you were biking over here?"

"Not a single one! I'm totally stumped. What am I going to do?" I buried my head in my hands.

"I'll bet my dads have a great idea. Right, Dads?"

Harold and the now-awake-and-upright Howard both nodded.

"Let's start with your parents' first date," Howard suggested. Clyde started taking notes down. "It was at Bangers and Mosh, right?"

"How did you know that?" I asked, amazed.

"Everyone in Royal Woods knows that, Lincoln," Harold said.

"Your mom was a crossing guard, and your dad was recently back from studying abroad in the United Kingdom," Howard said.

"Your mom slipped a secret admirer note in his back pocket," Harold added.

"They laughed for hours over Yorkshire pudding and roast beef."

"Classic," Clyde swooned.

This was getting way too mushy for me.

"I've heard the story a million times, but I didn't realize everyone else in town had, too!" I said.

"It's one of my favorites," Howard said. "I hear your Pop-Pop retells it every other Thursday down at Sunset Canyon to anyone who will listen."

"Lincoln, you have a great point," Harold said. *I did?* He continued, "If everyone in town knows the story of Rita and Lynn's first date, we should definitely have a huge, blowout party to celebrate!"

"Hare-bear, this really seems like the kind of event better suited for a small group. You know, family and close friends only."

"It's a love worth celebrating! We should be shouting from the rooftops!"

"But we can celebrate that big in a close-knit way," Howard said.

"Lincoln, they're your parents. You know them best. Why don't you choose the kind of party we should have?" Harold asked me.

I didn't know what to do. Would it be better to take Harold's advice and have a big party? If the past has shown me anything, big parties can have even bigger problems. Would it be better to take Howard's advice and have a small party? Or would that maybe feel *too* small? I knew I had to make a decision, and I'd have to trust that whatever decision I made would be the right decision.

It felt silly to be so nervous. And about a party, of all things! My parents weren't expecting anything from us. I just wanted to do something good for them. I probably should've just volunteered at the animal shelter or picked up litter from the beach instead. But it was too late to turn back now.

I looked back and forth between Harold and Howard. *Big party or little party? Big party or little party?* I decided to give them the most honest version of my answer.

"I mean, I'd love to throw them a huge party, and if I had more time, I think I could totally figure out how to do it. But their anniversary is today. There's no *way* I can get that together in time!"

"Never say never, Lincoln," Harold said with a wink. "Kindness goes a long way. Let me make a phone call to my old buddy Duke from college."

Harold jogged out of the kitchen, and I heard a door close.

"Who's Duke?" I asked.

"Never mind that for now. We need to talk about logistics," Howard said frantically.

"Right on top of it, Dad!" Clyde said, holding up the pen and pad.

"I can't believe I'm going to say this after the girls nearly gave me a nervous breakdown, but for this to work, we're going to need all of your sisters," Howard said. "At least the ones who are potty-trained."

"Well, they're not really talking to me right now," I replied. "I kind of messed up earlier, and they all got pretty mad at me. Especially Lana, Lynn, and Lucy. They were going to help me, but I got frustrated with them and they left."

"You're going to have to figure out how to fix all of that. They're your family. If you let them know that you're truly sorry, they will probably forgive you. That's what families do."

"You're right, Mr. McBride." I started gathering my stuff. "I'll go find them all."

"Wait just one sec," Howard said. "Let's see what Hare-bear finds out first."

We sat for a minute in silence at the table. I didn't want to be disrespectful to Mr. McBride, but it felt like we were wasting time by waiting, especially since I had to track down my sisters and beg for their forgiveness. Each passing second felt like forever. The cats, Cleopawtra and Nepurrtiti, scratched their scratching post in time with the ticking clock. I felt like I was going to jump out of my skin! Howard could tell we were feeling tense.

"So, are you boys excited for that new Ace Savvy movie?"

Clyde and I were about to respond when Harold burst back into the kitchen.

"Big news!" Harold said. "Duke said we're all set!"

"Of course Duke came through," Howard said with relief. "He's always been the most reliable friend we have."

"It's true. We've always been able to count on Duke."

"*Who is Duke?*" I said. I was worried I sounded a little impatient, but it felt like I was missing a major piece of the puzzle.

"Duke's my dads' friend from college," Clyde said. I shrugged. Clyde's dads were very popular in college. They participated in every activity and still have a lot of friends from back then. Duke could be their favorite antique dealer, or the person they were supposed to get that credenza from, for all I knew. His name meant nothing to me.

"He owns Bangers and Mosh. I called him to ask if we could get a discount on renting out the restaurant," Harold said.

Oh, *that* Duke. Of course.

"Holy cow! That's amazing. What did he say?" I asked.

"Well, like the rest of Royal Woods, he

knows your parents had their first date there, and they've had several dates there since. Since he knows your parents pretty well, and he didn't have any reservations for tonight, he's letting us have the space *for free*."

"That's incredible!"

"Wow, Dad! Way to go!"

"So, while you get your sisters, the three of us will start setting up the space. We have a whole box of British-themed decorations in the attic that should do the trick. I know I put that Union Jack bunting in a box somewhere."

"You should probably find Lori first. If I had to pick one of your sisters to curate a guest list and start making phone calls, I'd definitely pick her," Howard advised.

"Plus, she's the only Loud kid who knows how to drive," Clyde added.

"Are you sure I need to get *all* of my sisters to come help?" I was nervous that some of them may be a little less forgiving than Lori. "What if I just get a few of them? Or maybe one or two?"

"Lincoln, there are eleven of you and three of us. If three or four of us try to put this party together, there's no way we'd be done in time. If all fourteen of us are working on it, there's no way we can fail. You understand that, right?"

I thought I understood. I really hoped my sisters would understand, too. I was mostly thinking about Lynn, Lana, and Lucy. They really put a lot of effort into helping me earlier today. Even though it wasn't ideal, maybe I should've gone with that instead. Right now, we could've been eating vanilla with chocolate-covered pickles and rainbow sprinkles ice cream with my parents, while Lucy played a tune on the pipe organ.

"OK, Mr. McBride," I said. "I'll find my sisters and get them over to Bangers and Mosh as quickly as possible so we can get this party started. Thank you both again for helping me. This is going to be way better than a cricket circus and a cat card!"

Howard was right that Lori was the first sister I had to find. Not only would she be able to help me find our other siblings, but she also had Vanzilla today. (Mom and Dad always walked on Saturdays to make sure they got their steps in.) Lori's been working on her skills to go to Fairway University for college, so I knew exactly where she'd be.

I got off my bike quickly at Hole in One-derland, the mini-golf place in Royal Woods. Lori goes there a lot to practice her putting. Even though it's usually pretty busy on Saturdays, she still spends a lot of her weekends there. I ducked behind bridges and dodged moving arms and legs until I finally found her on the twelfth hole.

"Lori!" I exclaimed. That startled her, and she accidentally shanked her ball off the side of the windmill and into the water.

"What do you want, Lincoln? Can't you see I'm perfecting my short game?"

"I'm really sorry about this morning. I should've been more prepared when I woke you all up. But now Clyde's dads are helping put together a party for Mom and Dad at

Bangers and Mosh, and it won't work without all of us."

"Didn't they put together that concert in honor of Mayor Davis?"

"Yeah, in less than a week," I replied.

"And they did that thing for the reopening of the west side of the mall, right?"

"They even got Reininger's to give out free samples of that shampoo you like."

"Apple Rain Dream—my favorite!"

"Yeah, that one!"

"And it's going to be at Bangers and Mosh?"

"Yeah, they pulled some strings. So, with Clyde's dads helping us—"

"Say no more! I am *definitely* in for whatever they have planned," she said, putting her putter away. "They are literally the best party planners in all of Royal Woods. Come on,

Lincoln. Let's go find the rest of our sisters."

On the ride over to find our other sisters, I told Lori about the McBrides suggesting she put together the guest list, and she was on board instantly. She thought we should pick up Leni, Luna, and Luan next, and I agreed. They were only frustrated about the lack of a plan this morning, rather than the idea as a whole, so getting them to agree to it seemed a little easier.

Lori started listing names of all these people I'd never even heard of to invite to our parents' party. I did my best to write them all down for her as we headed to the Royal Woods Mall. I didn't think Principal Huggins needed to be on the list, but I realized ten of us had gone to Royal Woods Elementary School, so he probably knew my parents pretty well by now.

Seymour from Sunset Canyon was an odd choice, too, but I guessed Lori was adding him to the list because of Pop-Pop.

We parked in the mall parking lot and rushed inside. Even though she wasn't scheduled to work today, we quickly found Leni at her job: Reininger's department store.

"I'm not even on an assigned shift. I just felt like helping fold sweaters!" Leni said. Leni is the kind of person who just likes to help. We needed someone like that to make this party happen.

"Do you think you can come help us instead?" I asked.

"Totes! Let me just let Mrs. Carmichael know I'm going on lunch!"

"But Leni, you're not even supposed to be here today," Lori reminded her.

"Oh, then I'd better tell her I'm clocking out for the day!"

Lori and I knew we should just let it go and let Leni be Leni. Once we got in the car, I explained to Leni why we needed her and our other sisters to throw the ultimate party.

"O-M-Gosh, I was totes going to suggest we throw the party at Bangers and Mosh! There's no better way to celebrate your first date by having it all over again! But, if it's your first date again, is that like your second date? Or your first-first date?"

"Let's just turn the radio on," Lori suggested.

"Ooh, I love this song!"

Leni blasted her and Lori's favorite song, "Ooh Girl" by Boyz Will Be Boyz, and we drove to pick up another sister. Our next stop was the Burnt Bean, where Luna was practicing with her band. Lori parked the car, and the three of us ran to the stage.

"Hey, siblings, are you here to jam?" Luna asked. She played a loud solo on her guitar. Lori found the amp and switched it off.

"Whoa, what gives? I don't come into your life and turn off—um—your golf clubs, or whatever."

"That doesn't even make sense, Lunes," Lori said.

"You know what I mean!"

Sensing a fight, I had to step in quickly.

"Hey, Luna, I'm sorry about this morning. I know I confused everyone and it wasn't fair to wake everyone up without a plan, so I apologize."

"That's OK, little bro. It's just a tiny bit of

sleep. No rest for the wicked, anyway, right?"

"O-M-Gosh, Luna! Lincoln totes has a plan to celebrate Mom and Dad's anniversary," Leni added. "And it doesn't sound lame! But from everything Lori and Lincoln have said, it sounds like we need you in order to make it happen. I think we're going to need your band, too."

"You're going to need the band, eh? Let me see how the band feels about that. You guys want to play an impromptu gig?" Luna asked her bandmates. Sam, Mazzy, Sully, and Chunk, their roadie, all nodded. "Right on! OK, dudes, we're in!"

Lori dropped Leni and Luna and her band off at Bangers and Mosh. I stayed in the car with her to get our other sisters. We were wondering where we might find our youngest sister

Lily, until we got to the Chortle Portal comedy club to pick up Luan. There, we found Luan onstage wearing Lily in a baby carrier. Lily was taking a nap.

"And to the guy who invented zero? Thanks for nothing!" Luan said with a bow. The audience laughed and Lily seemed to wake up a little.

"You think numbers are funny, huh? Well, why was six afraid of seven?" Luan continued.

"Why?" the audience yelled back.

"Because seven *eight* nine!"

To our surprise, the audience laughed hard at Luan's joke. We'd been hearing that one around the house since before Luan even had braces.

"Thank you, you've been a lovely audience. I'll catch you again at the six o'clock show!"

The whole room applauded and hollered for Luan. She took a bow and left the stage. We met her at the side of the stage by a water fountain as she was pouring a cup for herself.

"Hi, guys, *water* you doing here? Ha-ha-ha! Get it?" she said, her cup splashing. Lily rolled her eyes.

"I'm really sorry about this morning," I said.

"Don't be! I ended up getting here early! This is my second set of the day already, and the audience is loving it!"

"Well, now we need you to come with us," Lori said.

"But I'm going on again in a little bit!" Luan said. "There's no way I'm missing the opportunity to have three comedy sets in one day!"

"Come on, Luan, it's for Mom and Dad," Lori insisted.

"You know they would understand. Funny is my business!"

Lori and I exchanged a glance. This was going to take more convincing than we'd expected.

"Clyde's dads helped get us a venue for an anniversary party. A real venue—with a stage! We're having the party at Bangers and Mosh. You can do at least one set there! Maybe even two!"

"You should've lead with that, toots!" Luan said through her ventriloquist dummy, Mr. Coconuts.

"So, you're in?" I asked.

"Bangers and Mosh is at least *twice* the size of this place. Of *course* I'm in!"

"Great, let's go!" Lori said as she grabbed Luan's arm. The four of us and Mr. Coconuts dashed back out to Vanzilla.

"So, how'd you end up with Lily?" I asked.

"Mom and Dad came by my midday set. Your speech from this morning was stuck in my head all day, so when they came by, I offered to help them out with their errands. They said babysitting would be the most helpful thing I could do, and I told them I'd be happy to be of a-*sister*-ance! Get it?"

Lori and I groaned. Lily blew a raspberry.

Our next stop was at the observatory to pick up Lisa. We had to drive up a pretty winding road to get there, so there was no time to lose once we arrived. Inside, Lisa was surrounded by other scientists with clipboards and computers murmuring to one another.

"Apologies, siblings, but I've promised my fellow astronomers to wait until I can witness a Cepheid variable—or, in layman's terms, a variable star—pulsating in time to the latest Mick Swagger song."

Lori looked at all of us and shrugged.

"Come on, guys," she said. "How long could that possibly take?"

"It can take over thirty years for a star's rhythm to reach our atmosphere," Lisa said, adjusting her glasses.

Our eyes went wide.

"We don't have that kind of time, Lis!" I said.

"All of us need to help with the party," Lori added.

"Come on, Lisa! Just think of Mom and Dad's anniversary party as a space party," Luan said. "And there's only one way to throw a space party."

"And how does one throw a space party exactly?" Lisa inquired.

"You *planet*! Get it? Ha-ha-ha-ha!" Luan laughed.

"We'll get her to stop telling jokes if you come help us with Mom and Dad's party," Lori offered.

"Deal," Lisa said, grabbing her clipboard and various other scientific equipment.

Our next stop was the Royal Woods recreational center, to get Lola. She was teaching a class on how to smile and wave for girls who were new to pageants. We knew it would be super hard to pull her from what she was doing—she's easily the most stubborn of all of us—so we were prepared to negotiate.

"You interrupted my beauty sleep this morning, and now you're asking for a favor?" Lola asked, looking over her shoulder at the group of girls practicing their waves and smiles. "Come on, Iris! You can smile wider than that!"

"Lola, it's not a favor for *us*—it's a favor for Mom and Dad!" I said.

"*You're* the ones asking me to leave these poor, unfortunate crown-less and wave-less girls to spend my time on some party plan Lincoln came up with last minute that will almost definitely fail. What's in it for me?"

"You wouldn't have a single crown or sash if you didn't have Mom and Dad to take you to your pageants," Lori said.

"Ugh, I hate when you're right," Lola said. She turned back to her class. "OK, girls, that's enough for today. We'll pick it up next week."

"How'd you do that?" I whispered to Lori.

"It's called being the oldest," she said, flipping her hair with her hand.

Lori and I made another stop at Bangers and Mosh to drop off Luan, Lily, Lola, and Lisa. We knew they'd be way more useful to the sisters setting up the party than to us in the van. I hoped everything was going smoothly at the restaurant. Clyde hadn't called me on my walkie-talkie, so I wasn't worried. If there was a problem, he would've called me at least a dozen times by now.

Our final stop was at our house. It was time to apologize to Lucy, Lynn, and Lana. I explained to Lori on the way what happened earlier, and I hoped they'd be able to forgive me. Luckily, they were still at home in the backyard. Lana and Lucy were working on digging techniques, and Lynn was doing some kind of training exercise.

I walked over to them, dodging a football Lynn threw toward me.

"Hi, guys," I said. Lori came up next to me and put her hand on my shoulder.

"What's Stinkin' doing here?" Lynn asked Lori.

"You're dead to us," Lucy said. "That's usually a good thing for me, but in this case, it's not."

"My crickets told me not to talk to you," Lana said, crossing her arms and turning around.

"You guys, give him a chance to speak," Lori said. "He knows he messed up and he wants to make it up to you. Go ahead, Lincoln. Tell them what you told me."

"I'm really sorry about how I treated you all earlier. I was a total jerk."

"True that," Lana said.

"But now Clyde's dads are helping us out and we're all setting up a really awesome party for Mom and Dad at Bangers and Mosh. But there's no way it will be awesome without you three there. Do you guys think you can forgive me and come help us throw what might actually be the ultimate anniversary party for Mom and Dad?"

My sisters looked at one another without making a sound. It was almost as if they were speaking their own language. Finally, Lucy spoke up.

"We'll do it, if you do our chores for three weeks and give us each one week of your allowance."

"SERIOUSLY?!" I shouted.

"LINCOLN!" Lori yelled at me.

"What about two weeks of chores and you guys split one week of my allowance?"

Lynn spit in her hand and offered it to me to shake.

"It's a deal, Stinkin'. Now, when does this party start?"

The five of us hugged and ran back to Vanzilla. I couldn't believe it. This morning, it was total typical Loud family chaos. Now, all eleven of us were coming together to throw a party that sounded way cooler than anything I could ever have come up with on my own. I was going to have to figure out a way to make money over the next few weeks since my sisters called dibs on my allowance, but it was worth it if this was going to make my parents happy.

Lori, Lynn, Lucy, Lana, and I walked into the restaurant. It was already totally transformed. For the first time all day, I felt like we were actually doing the right thing. After the fish oil incident, I swore to myself I'd follow my parents' request to avoid party planning, but as I looked over the cool stuff my sisters and the

McBrides were setting up, I felt really good about not going with my gut. They'd even set up a photo booth for people to take pictures. My dad *loves* photo booths. This was going to be awesome!

"O-M-Gosh, Lincoln, can you believe it?" Leni asked as she pinned a streamer to the wall. "We're in a restaurant without any people in it! Isn't that wild?"

"Leni, we're literally at Dad's restaurant without customers all the time," Lori said, shaking her head. "But good job, Lincoln! Mom and Dad are going to love it."

"Thanks, Lori. But the real thanks go to the McBrides. They did more in two hours than I could've imagined doing in two weeks!"

"Thank you, Mr. and Mr. McBride!" all eleven of us shouted at once.

"Our work is just beginning," Howard said, handing me a broom and a dustpan. "We have everything ready to go. Lori, you worked to get our guest list in order. Luna and her band have already put together their set list for their performance tonight, Luan has her stand-up routine in order, and Lola's ribbon dance is looking perfect. Lisa and Lynn are creating an incredible scientifically tested menu, and Lucy, Lana, and Leni are making this place look very cool and celebratory. Lincoln and Lily, keep helping everyone clean up and make things perfect."

"You're all doing a really great job," Harold chimed in. "Clyde has been checking off our list and it looks like we're just about ready to open doors to our guests. Just a few more minutes of setting up and sweeping!"

Luna and her band played a song as we all continued working together to set up Bangers and Mosh as the perfect party spot. I was still amazed that Clyde's dads were able to make this happen, but as I saw Lucy, Leni, and Lana string up Union Jack bunting across the room, I became even more excited.

When you're part of a big family, you hear the same stories over and over. The story we hear over and over is how our parents met and when they started dating. That all started here. There would be no Loud family without Bangers and Mosh, so getting to throw this party in this restaurant was super special. Even Lisa, the one Loud who never gets emotional, wiped a tear from her eye as we were setting the party up.

Lynn and Lisa put together the perfect

menu. It was bite-sized versions of all of Mom and Dad's favorite British foods, including fish and chips, Yorkshire pudding, shepherd's pie, Scotch eggs, toad in the hole, and even sticky toffee pudding. Clyde helped me and Lily clean up and move the tables so we'd have a dance floor and a buffet table. Between the changed setup and the decorations my sisters were putting up, it looked like the ideal transformation of a regular restaurant into an amazing party venue—especially for two people who really liked Bangers and Mosh (aka my parents).

Lori had done a great job of putting together the guest list. Just as we had brushed away the last dust bunny, people started coming into the restaurant. Pop-Pop and Myrtle were the first to arrive. Then

Dr. Feinstein, my mom's boss and our dentist, came, too, followed by a busload full of seniors from Sunset Canyon, including Scoots, Seymour, and Bernie; my dad's childhood home-ec teacher Mildred Scalise; my dad's best friend, Kotaro; Grant, the waiter from my dad's restaurant; Flip; Mr. Grouse; my teacher, Mrs. Johnson; Librarian Wetta—every single adult in Royal Woods seemed to be there!

Our parents' friends helped us finish up the cleaning and decorating. They even helped Luna and her band with their sound check. When it looked like everything was pretty much done, Harold picked up a fork and clinked a glass to get everyone's attention.

"Hi, folks. Thank you all for coming out tonight," Harold said. "Rita and Lynn

Loud Sr. are both important people to everyone in this room. We appreciate how quickly you all responded, especially given the extremely short notice. There's a guest book at the front that we'd love for you to sign, and a photo booth over by the statue of the Beefeater. Rita and Lynn don't expect this. They don't know that any of this is happening. We just need someone to pick them up and bring them here."

Everyone applauded in agreement. I looked around the room. Everyone was smiling and excited. Even the grumpier people like Mr. Grouse and Scoots were grinning. It was so cool to see so many people there just to celebrate my parents.

"I'll happily bring Rita and Lynn to their party," Duke, the owner of Bangers and Mosh, said. "After all, it's this very place that brought them together for the first time."

"Hear, hear!" the crowd cheered in response.

"Nah, Chief," Flip said. "These folks once taught ol' Flip about the meaning of Thanksgiving. I'll happily pick 'em up."

"Flip, really," Duke insisted. "It would be my honor."

"Honor, schmonor. Let me get 'em."

"I must insist."

"'Ey buddy, I said I got 'em."

Duke gave Harold a look, and Harold responded with a shrug. The thing about Flip is that we all know he's a bit of a hustler, and he's kind of strange. He rarely keeps his word, and he's not a very trustworthy person. Every once in a while, he could surprise you, but he was basically the last person we wanted to pick up our parents. He also didn't seem to be giving in right now.

"Fine, Flip. Go ahead," Harold said.

The crowd, including me and my sisters, all gasped as Flip walked out the door.

"I'm not sure that was your best decision," Howard whispered to Harold.

"Me neither," Harold said, checking his watch. "But the good news is, we have plenty of time until the party officially starts."

For a few minutes, we all touched up the decorations and worked together to set out the food for my parents' arrival. Every single Union Jack was in its right place. In a million years, I couldn't have imagined a party that looked like this. I made a mental note to write a thank-you card for Howard and Harold. I

made a second mental note to make sure I found the card at anywhere other than Flip's Food and Fuel.

We all kept watching the top of the stairs leading into the restaurant, waiting impatiently for my parents' arrival.

The handle on the door jiggled. The crowd froze. Flip appeared in the doorway at the top of the stairs, blocking the entrance. He raised a finger to his lips and shushed us all. We waited, our eyes wide.

"And now announcing the moment you've all been waiting for—but it's gonna cost ya," Flip said. Harold rolled his eyes and took out his wallet. "*Buuuuuuuuuuuuuuurrrrrrrrrrpppppp. Here's the happy, sappy couple!*"

We all cheered. Just as my sister Lisa dropped the "Happy Anniversary" banner, the crowd went quiet. A couple who was happy to celebrate at Bangers and Mosh came through the door and stood at the top of the stairs . . . but that couple was clearly not our parents.

"Wow, Mom and Dad look really different!" Leni said. "Congratulations, Mom and Dad!"

"Leni, those aren't our parents," Lori said.

"What is happening?" I asked Harold nervously. "Who are they?"

"I'll handle this," Harold said to me. "Flip! That's not Rita and Lynn!" Harold yelled. Howard immediately fainted.

"Who?" Flip said, scratching his butt. "You asked for a couple celebrating their anniversary, so I brought you a couple celebrating their anniversary. Now, where's my twenty bucks?"

"You're not getting squat," Harold said.

"Fine, then I'm taking these people back to Jean Juan's French-Mex Buffet."

"Fine. Happy anniversary, folks."

Flip left with the bewildered couple. Honestly, I'm not sure why they decided to go back with Flip. They should've just asked to stay here.

Duke walked up to Harold. "I've got this," he said with a smile.

"Thank you," Harold said as he lifted Howard up onto a chair. We reset the banner and got back into our places. Duke would have no trouble finding our real parents, and he probably wouldn't charge Mr. McBride twenty dollars to pick them up, either.

After the last false start, everyone was quiet as we waited for my parents to come through the door. I stood with all of my sisters.

"I can't believe we might actually pull this off," I said.

"And in one day!" Lori added.

"Maybe that was the problem before," Luna

asked. "We were overthinking the whole thing."

We all gave Luna a look. We knew there was no way we could've pulled this off without Clyde's dads.

"Or we just needed the McBrides. Whatever," Luna said, plucking her guitar.

"Hey, guys, it's almost *thyme* to party!" Luan said, thrusting herbs out in front of our faces. We groaned in response.

The doorknob jiggled again. This time, Duke appeared in the doorway. He shushed us, and we all went totally silent.

"It'd better be Mom and Dad this time," Lola whispered. "I could be practicing my ribbon dancing right now."

"*Shhhh!*" Lily said to Lola.

Duke led our blindfolded parents to the top

of the stairs. They were dressed in their date-night clothing, so he must've told them they were doing *something* special. We all looked at one another excitedly. Duke untied their blind-folds at the same time. Mom and Dad looked completely shocked. *Yes!*

"SURPRISE!!!! HAPPY ANNIVER-SARY!!!" everyone shouted. Lisa once again lowered the "Happy Anniversary" banner my sisters had made earlier.

Luna joined her band onstage and started rocking out, playing one of Mom and Dad's favorite romantic songs from when they first started dating. Our parents walked down the stairs. My dad is the most emotional person ever, and he immediately started sobbing. I even saw my mom wipe away a tear or two, though she's pretty good at holding it together. I watched them take in the crowd. They were clearly speechless and surprised by how many friends and family members came out to celebrate.

"Thank—*waahhh*—yoooou—*waahhhhh*—everyone!" my dad said between big sobs. "We—*waahhh*—love—*waahhhhh*—you!"

My mom held his hand.

"Gosh, you guys, it's not even our sapphire year yet!"

"I told you so," I heard Harold whisper to Howard.

"SPEECH! SPEECH! SPEECH! SPEECH!" everyone chanted. My dad could barely stop sniffling, so Harold handed my mom a microphone.

"We appreciate you all so very much. Thank you for being part of this complete surprise!

We were just going to order a pizza from Spunk E. Pigeon's Pizza Palooza Paradise and watch a rerun of *The Dream Boat*, but instead, we find ourselves here, surrounded by all of our family and friends—"

"—and some people I definitely don't recognize," my dad said quietly. My mom raised her eyebrow at him.

"As you may know, we had our first date here many years ago—"

"We know!" everyone shouted. My mom and dad laughed.

"Yes, you all know. Anyway, thank you for coming out. Let's eat some great food and listen to some rock music! Woo!" Mom made the "rock on" hand gesture and stuck out her tongue, which made her look just like Luna, and everyone laughed.

People started chatting again. Scoots immediately rolled up to the dessert table and started stuffing sticky toffee puddings into her purse. Pop-Pop and Myrtle skipped over to the dance floor. Kotaro joined Luna and her band onstage with his cowbell.

Mom and Dad walked up to Howard and Harold.

"Did you guys do this?" Dad asked.

"Thank you so much," Mom said.

"Oh, we didn't do this," Harold said, winking at Howard.

"We helped a little," Howard added. "But it was Lincoln who asked us to help. Without him and all of your daughters, there'd be no party."

"All of your kids wanted to celebrate with you."

We gathered around and Dad started sobbing again. Luan handed him her novelty clowning scarf so he could blow his nose.

"There, there, Lynn," Mom said, patting Dad on the back. "Thank you both so much, Howard and Harold. This is really spectacular."

"You're welcome," Harold said. He and Howard hugged Mom and Dad. "Come on, Howie. This is our song."

Harold and Howard walked over to the dance floor, leaving us together. Luna handed her guitar to her roadie, Chunk, and came down off the stage to join us.

"Wow, you guys," Mom said to all eleven of us. "We're both so impressed and just so touched."

"I . . ." Dad started. Another flood of tears hit him, and he crumbled to the ground.

"We know, Dad," Lori said kindly, touching his shoulder.

"If it weren't for Lincoln, none of this would've happened. We wanted to avoid doing anything, since we didn't want a repeat of the banana pudding incident," Lola added.

"He was screaming about some 'ultimate anniversary party' and reminding us of all the really cool things you guys do for us all day," Lynn said. "And once there was a plan, we were fully on board to join the team!"

"It seems like you broke the curse," Mom said. "Even Aunt Ruth is having a good time!"

We all looked at Aunt Ruth. She was getting down on the dance floor with Flip and her cats. I wasn't quite sure how Flip came back so quickly, but I was happy to see everyone having a great time.

"Thanks, kids," our mom said as she pulled us in for a big hug.

Somehow, after all of the bonkers events of the day, we'd been able to pull off the ultimate party. Sure, there were some weird moments— mostly with Flip—but Mom was right: We'd finally broken the curse.

The party went on for hours. Everyone danced and ate and celebrated. It was perfect, and my sisters and I would always remember tonight as one of those times we came together and made something amazing happen for our mom and dad.